panda series

**PANDA books are for first readers
beginning to make their own way
through books.**

Lighthouse Joey

Written and illustrated by
• MARIE BURLINGTON •

THE O'BRIEN PRESS
DUBLIN

First published 2006 by The O'Brien Press Ltd,
12 Terenure Road East, Rathgar, Dublin 6, Ireland.
Tel: +353 1 4923333; Fax: +353 1 4922777
E-mail: books@obrien.ie
Website: www.obrien.ie
Reprinted 2006, 2007.

ISBN: 978-0-86278-945-9

British Library Cataloguing-in-Publication Data
Burlington, Marie
Lighthouse Joey. - (Panda books ; 33)
1.Boots - Juvenile fiction 2.Treasure troves - Juvenile fiction
3.Pirates - Juvenile fiction 4.Children's stories
I.Title
823.9'2[J]

3 4 5 6 7 8 9
07 08 09 10

The O'Brien Press receives
assistance from

the arts council
schomhairle
ealaíon

Typesetting, layout, editing, design: The O'Brien Press Ltd.
Printed and bound in the UK by J.H. Haynes & Co Ltd, Sparkford

Can YOU spot the panda
hidden in the story?

High on the rocks
at the edge of
an old fishing village
stands a lighthouse.

This is where Joey lives
with his Mum and Dad
and his pet seagull, Skipper.

The lighthouse has five rooms.
Inside it looks like this.

Joey found Skipper
when he was out one day
collecting shells.

The seagull was a
very young bird
and had a damaged wing.
It hopped along the sand.
'CAW, CAW,'
cried the little bird.

'Wait here,' said Joey.
'I'll go and get you
something to eat.'
Joey brought scraps of food.
Then the young seagull
followed him home.

'Can I keep him, Mum?'
begged Joey. 'Can I? Please.'
'We'll see,' said Mum.
That usually meant yes.

Joey made a bed for Skipper
out of a box and some straw.
He put it under his window.
Skipper settled in.

This was his home now.
He could still fly a little bit
but not too far.

Joey loved living
in the lighthouse.
He loved the sound of the sea
going '**swish**, **swish**'
under his window.
It lulled him to sleep at night.

Every night the large
beam of light
from the lighthouse
cut through the darkness
like a magical sword.

It guided ships at sea
and kept them safe
from rocks and danger.

Joey knew that each lighthouse
had its own special signal.
This told sailors
where they were.

Joey's was: **one flash
every ten seconds**.

Joey often counted the seconds.

He would look for that signal
if he were lost at sea.
He would know then
he was near home.

And when the fog came
the foghorn sent out
its special sound.
It warned the ships where
the dangerous rocks were.

Joey's best friend Danny
said it sounded like a
sick cow.
But Joey loved
the comforting noise.
He felt warm and safe
in his bed.

'I like living in a proper house
with a garden,' said Danny.
But Joey was happy
in his lighthouse home.
The sea was *his* garden.

Joey's dad was
the lighthouse keeper.
He had to look after
all the equipment.
He fixed anything that broke.
He wrote a report every day.

Joey's dad's job
was very important.
The sailors depended on him.

Every morning Joey watched
the sailing boats and
the fishing boats go out to sea.
In the late evening
he watched them return again.
He hoped they would be safe.

Nearby was the beach.
The rocks and caves
echoed with the
memories of the sea.
Joey knew all its
stories and legends.

Joey and Danny often
pretended to be the pirates
Jumping Jack
and his mate.
The old stories said that
Jumping Jack's treasure
was buried in the biggest cave.

25

They went into
Jumping Jack's cave.
'AAARGH, ME HEARTIES!'
they shouted.
'AAARGH, ME HEARTIES!'

HEARTIES

HEARTIES

HEARTIES

HEARTIES

HEARTIES

HEARTIES

HEARTIES

HEARTIES

the cave echoed back.

One night a storm blew up.
Joey looked out his window.
The wild waves crashed
against the shore.
Joey could see the lights
of the houses in the harbour.

Suddenly he saw
a strange light.

A small beam was swinging
back and forth near
Jumping Jack's cave.
Very strange, thought Joey,
that looks like a **lantern**.
But nobody used lanterns
anymore.

Had **Jumping Jack** come back from the past to search for his treasure?

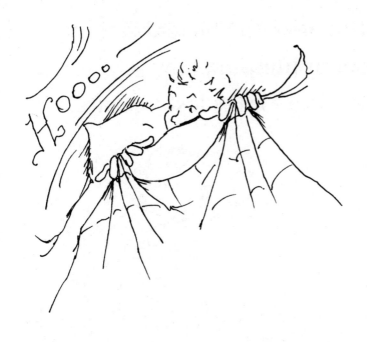

Joey felt really scared.
He jumped into bed and
pulled the covers over his head.
'HOOOO,' went the wind.
Joey shivered.

The next day he told Danny
about Jumping Jack
looking for his lost treasure.

'Let's see if **we** can find it first,'
said Danny.
Joey and Danny
searched the beach and caves.

They wore their favourite
pirate outfits.
They were the world's
scariest pirates.

They screamed their worst
bloodcurdling screams.

They found **driftwood**
and **shells** and **stones**.
Joey added them to his
collection on his window sill.
But they did not find
any treasure.

But on his way home,
Joey found something strange.
It was a pair of boots.
Old boots. **Very old** boots.

They were stuck in the sand
near the lighthouse.
Were they
Jumping Jack's boots?

The next morning
Joey and Skipper
went to the cave
to check on the boots.
But the boots were gone.

Very strange, Joey thought.
Maybe **Jumping Jack**
was hanging around
somewhere?
He looked along the beach.
He looked at the rocks.
Nobody.

'Come on, Skipper,'
he said, 'let's go.'
But Skipper was pulling
at something.
It was stuck
between the rocks
just inside the cave.

Joey went to see. 'WOW!'
It was a big, old **key**.
Was it the key to
Jumping Jack's treasure chest?

Joey ran home and
showed the key to
Mum and Dad.

'Maybe it opens a door,'
said Mum.
Dad knew all the
old places in the town.

They tried the door
of the **old church**.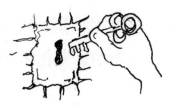

They tried the door
of the **old prison**.

They tried the doors
of the **old cottages**.

But the key did not work.

Joey put the key
with his collection.

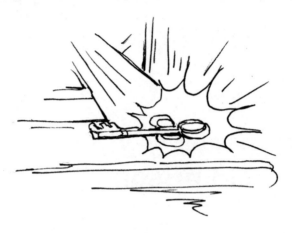

One night, as the moon
shone in his window,
Joey saw the key
twinkling in the light.
Were there any old places
they hadn't tried?

There's one place, he thought.
Here! Here in our
own lighthouse.

The next day he went
down to the storeroom.
It was under the lighthouse.
Dad used it as his workshop.

He found what
he was looking for
under a pile of wooden boxes.
It was a trapdoor
with a big, round, metal ring
on top.

Joey moved the wooden boxes.
He grabbed the handle
of the big trapdoor.
He pulled and pulled.

At last the old trapdoor opened.

There were steps going down.
Was there something
down here that
Skipper's key would open?

Joey took down the torch
that hung beside
the storeroom door.

It was dark and
the steps were slippery.

Down he went until he came
to a long passageway.
He crept forward slowly.
Water dripped down
from the roof.

Suddenly the passageway
opened out
in different directions.
Which way should he go?
Joey could not see a thing.

I should go back, he thought.
But which way *was* back?
Am I **lost**? he thought.

Then he heard
a noise somewhere.
What was that?
Was it **Jumping Jack**?
Wait, it was Skipper.
'CAW, CAW,' Joey heard.

Skipper must have hopped
along the beach.
He must be at
the other side of the caves.

'CAW, CAW,' cried Skipper,
telling Joey which way to go.
'**CAW**, **CAW**.'
'I'm here, Skipper,'
shouted Joey.

Skipper hopped and flew
outside and
Joey listened and
followed his cry.

Soon Joey came to
the last cave.
And there, hidden in the rocks,
was a wooden trunk.
The treasure!

'HERE, SKIPPER,' he shouted.
Skipper found a small gap
in the roof of the cave.
He hopped in.

Joey took out the key
and put it in the keyhole.
It fitted perfectly.
He turned it gently.
He opened the trunk.

Inside, wrapped in faded cloth
was a scroll.
It was tied with a ribbon.
Joey raced back
to show it to Mum and Dad.

They were angry with Joey
for going into the caves.
But they were excited too
to see the scroll.
They took it to the museum.

The curator was amazed.
He opened the scroll carefully.
It was a map of the old town.
There were lots of arrows on it.
'Wait,' he said.

He followed the arrows
with his finger.
'The map leads here,
right under our noses,
I mean right under our **feet**.
Imagine, Jumping Jack's
treasure was **here**
all the time.'

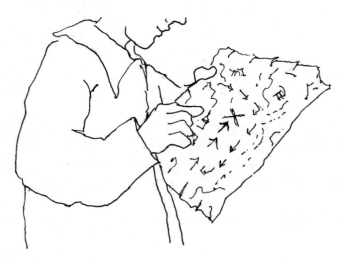

They lifted some of
the old stone slabs
in the big hall of the museum
and **there it was**.

**A large box
covered in
precious jewels.**

Inside were lots of
gold coins.

The box was placed
in the museum.
It was the best treasure
ever found in the village.

The museum had two copies
of Skipper's key made.
One large one for Joey
and one small one for Skipper.

Their pictures
appeared in the papers.

LIGHTHOUSE JOEY AND SEAGULL SKIPPER

FIND PIRATE'S TREASURE

ran the headlines.

Lots of tourists came
to visit the town.
They took pictures of
Joey and Skipper and
looked in Jumping Jack's cave.

Joey never did find out who owned the old boots.

Maybe they were **Jumping Jack's** boots, after all?